Published by
GRANDREAMS LIMITED
435-437 Edgware Road, Little Venice
London W2 1TH

Printed in Malaysia

50
BEDTIME
STORIES

Written by Anne McKie
Illustrated by Ken McKie

Contents

Dixie's Little Bag

Dixie loved playing with handbags and purses and shoulder bags. She had quite a collection. Her aunties and their girlfriends would give Dixie their old handbags. But the ones she liked best were those she had chosen for herself when she went shopping.

One afternoon when Dixie was in her room playing with some of her handbags, her Aunt Margot popped her head round the door.

"I need a little girl with a little bag to help me with my shopping!" she said with a smile. "Just a small bag will be fine. I have some very special shopping to do."

So Dixie chose her favourite red shoulder bag and off they went.

"I won't be able to put much shopping in here!" said Dixie to her aunt.

"Your red shoulder bag will be just perfect!" grinned Aunt Margot.

At the shops they bought a tiny round mirror, a jingling silver bell and the strangest wobbly toy, and they all fitted perfectly into Dixie's red shoulder bag.

"That's all the shopping I need," said Aunt Margot. "Let's go home!"

Now when Dixie opened her front door, she heard a loud chirping sound. There on the table was a beautiful blue budgerigar.

"It's for you, Dixie!" said her Aunt Margot. "Now you know why I needed a little girl with a little bag!"

8

The Midnight Monster

The night was dark, and the sky was full of twinkly stars as Ferdie Fox and little Byron Badger took a late stroll through Trudy's garden. Suddenly the moon came from behind a cloud.

"Look!" squealed Byron. "There's a monster on the lawn!"

"I do believe Ossie was laughing!" said Byron Badger, and the two frightened friends scampered home as fast as they could.

Next morning the sun was shining brightly and Trudy was playing on the lawn.

"I can't believe we could be so silly," whispered Ferdie, as he and the little badger peered through the bushes.

"How about coming back tonight to play?" giggled Byron, and he gave Ferdie a nudge. "We'll bring our own buckets and spades!"

"It wasn't there last night!" said Ferdie, his voice trembling as he grabbed little Badger's paw and they both dived into the nearest bush.

"Come back in the morning, you silly pair!" hooted Ossie Owl, and he fluttered off into the trees.

9

Pollyanna's Pockets

Pollyanna had lots of soft toys. She had a whole family of teddies, a giant giraffe, a great big elephant and no end of fluffy pink rabbits.

One birthday, Pollyanna's Gran gave her a tiny soft toy dog, just small enough to pop in her pocket.

Pollyanna liked her pocket toy so much, she asked for more at Christmas, and very soon she had enough to put into all her pockets.

Every night when she went to bed, Pollyanna put her tiny toys next to her pillow.

During the night, as Pollyanna turned over, some of the toys got lost in the bedclothes and she couldn't find them.

So the little girl had to call her mum and dad to help search for them. This happened several times every single night.

One morning, Gran called while Mum, Dad and Pollyanna were having breakfast. Pollyanna tucked into her cereal and toast, but Mum and Dad were falling asleep at the table.

"Why are you both so tired?" asked Gran in amazement.

"We've been up all night trying to find Pollyanna's pocket toys," yawned Dad when he heard Gran's voice.

"I've got the answer!" said Gran, rather loudly. "Lots and lots of pockets. That's what you need!"

So Gran went home and made a cushion with lots and lots of pockets, just enough for all Pollyanna's pocket toys.

Pollyanna keeps it at the side of her pillow. Now everyone gets a good night's sleep!

Jemima's New Outfit

Joanne had a favourite doll. Her name was Jemima. The little girl took her doll everywhere and always held onto her very tightly.

Joanne took Jemima shopping, she took her out into the garden, she took her to the park, and at the end of the day she took her to bed.

One afternoon Joanne went out to tea with her Gran, and Jemima went too.

"Whatever has happened to poor Jemima's dress?" asked Gran as she picked up Joanne's doll.

"Oh no!" cried the little girl. "There's a hole in the back and her hem is all torn. Whatever shall we do?"

"I'm afraid Jemima's dress is too thin to mend," Gran said, as she took a closer look. "Don't worry," she smiled. "Bring me that photograph in the silver frame."

"That's me when I was a baby," said Joanne.

"It's you on the day you were christened, and didn't you look beautiful," Gran laughed. "Now bring me that big cardboard box from the bottom drawer."

Inside the box was the prettiest dress Joanne had ever seen.

"This is the dress you are wearing in the photograph," said Gran, and she took it out and held it up. "Now let's see if it will fit Jemima!"

The tiny dress fitted perfectly, and when Joanne took another look inside the box, she found a little lace bonnet and a pair of the tiniest satin shoes.

"I'll take great care of these," promised the little girl, "and so will Jemima!"

Clumsy Claude Gets on Board

Claude was very, very clumsy. He tripped over everything in his house, and when he went outside everyone kept out of his way – just in case he fell over them.

One day Claude got a present from his mum, who didn't think he was clumsy at all!

"What is it?" asked Claude, as he showed it to his friends.

"Errm…it's a shopping trolley," said one.

"It's a flat board with wheels for moving heavy goods around," mumbled another.

"Great!" cried clumsy Claude. "It will come in really useful."

Now nobody, but nobody, dared tell Clumsy Claude that his present was really a skateboard…Claude on a skateboard…no-one would be safe!

So from then on, Claude used his 'special shopping trolley' to carry all sorts of things home for his friends.

In the summer, Claude took heavy cases to the train station for folks who were going on holiday. And at Christmas, Claude's special shopping trolley came in very useful for carrying presents and Christmas trees around…until one frosty morning…

Claude had just reached the top of the hill, for he was going into town to do some last-minute shopping. All of a sudden he tripped over his shoe lace, bumped into a lamp post, then fell backwards onto his special shopping trolley and went full speed down the hill into town.

Now as you can see, without even trying, Clumsy Claude very soon became a whizz on a skateboard. As he sped along, he did jumps and flips and spins and turns. He even flew upside-down. When he reached the bottom of the hill, his friends who had been watching started clapping and cheering.

"Clumsy Claude, King of the Skateboard!" they chanted.

"Oh, you mean my special shopping trolley," said Claude, looking a bit confused.

And he promptly fell off and flattened everything around him!

15

Mr Fox is up to his Tricks!

Bobby Rabbit was looking forward to his holiday – a whole week away in the sun. No work to do and definitely no Mr Fox to play tricks on him!

So just before it was time to catch the train, Bobby Rabbit threw all his holiday clothes into his suitcase, grabbed his umbrella (in case of rain), then reached for the key to lock his front door.

"Wait a minute!" said Bobby out loud. "I believe I hear water running. I must have a dripping tap." So he ran upstairs to check.

Now sly Mr Fox, who was hiding round the side of the house, saw Bobby Rabbit go back inside.

"This is the chance I've been waiting for!" Mr Fox sniggered. "I'll make quite sure that Bobby Rabbit never catches the train, and I'll go on holiday in his place."

…Now wasn't Mr Fox a nasty fellow?…

At last Bobby came dashing out of his house. He locked the front door, grabbed his suitcase and umbrella and ran down the path.

All of a sudden his suitcase flew open and poor Bobby's holiday clothes were scattered all over the place.

Sly Mr Fox had loosened the locks of course!

Then, much to Bobby Rabbit's surprise, it began to rain, although the sun was shining brightly. Can you guess who is behind the wall with the hose pipe? Sly Mr Fox of course!

"I mustn't get my holiday clothes wet!" cried Bobby Rabbit. So he put up his umbrella at once.

Poor Bobby, someone had filled his umbrella with soot, which fell all over him and his holiday clothes.

"It must be sly Mr Fox," sighed a very black Bobby Rabbit. "I should have known. No going on holiday for me now. I've missed the train and I shall have to stay at home."

But guess who jumped on the train as it left the station, and is going off for a whole week's holiday in the sun? Why, sly Mr Fox of course!

While Mr Fox was Away...

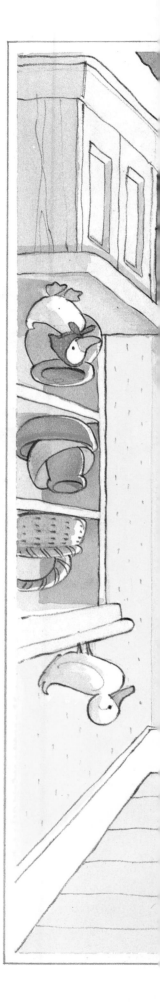

Try not to feel too sorry for Bobby Rabbit. He plays a far worse trick on Mr Fox, just wait and see!

"I now have a whole week to plan the biggest trick I have ever played on Mr Fox," said Bobby Rabbit to himself. "I'll give him going on holiday in my place!"

So Bobby made a big chocolate milkshake, sat down in his most comfortable chair, closed his eyes and thought very hard.

Next morning, Bobby Rabbit got out of bed as soon as it was light. He found it very hard to keep from giggling…the plan he had thought of was so brilliant.

First he looked into his tool box to make sure he had plenty of string and screws, and most important of all, a big tube of strong glue.

Then off went Bobby Rabbit to Mr Fox's house. He could hardly carry his heavy tool box, he was laughing so much!

Now Bobby knew exactly where Mr Fox kept his spare key (under a plant pot, right next to the front door). So he turned the key in the lock, hopped inside and started work at once.

It took a whole week of hard work, but a few minutes before Mr Fox returned from his holiday in the sun, Bobby Rabbit was finished!

Mr Fox opened his front door and gazed round the room in disbelief.

"I must be ill!" he gasped, trying to reach for a chair that was glued to the ceiling…for crafty Bobby Rabbit had turned the whole room UPSIDE-DOWN!

"It must be a nightmare!" yelled Mr Fox, as he ran screaming from his house.

But Bobby Rabbit didn't hear him, because he had just jumped on a train and was going for a whole month's holiday in the sun!

Mr Maggs Drives Monty

Little Mr Maggs had a big dog named Monty, who loved to go for lots and lots of walks. But Monty's legs were so long that Mr Maggs had to run to keep up with him.

After lunch one day Mr Maggs had a bright idea. "We'll drive out into the country, then you can run around the fields and get plenty of exercise," Mr Maggs told Monty.

So into the kitchen went little Mr Maggs. He made a flask of hot coffee for himself, and filled a bottle of water for Monty. Then he took a big packet of chocolate biscuits for them both to share while they were in the countryside that afternoon.

As they drove along, poor Mr Maggs had to squeeze up so tightly to Monty, he could hardly turn the steering wheel. And Monty didn't help one little bit. He kept licking Mr Maggs' ear, just to show how happy he was.

The car stopped at last. Monty leapt out, jumped over a gate and bounded round and round a big grassy field full of lovely buttercups and daisies.

Mr Maggs smiled as he watched Monty enjoying himself.

"Your dog is as big as me!" said a voice. It made Mr Maggs jump right off the ground.

Then from behind the hedge trotted a Shetland pony.

"I do believe he is!" laughed Mr Maggs.

Straightaway Monty bounded across to investigate. And when the Shetland pony and Monty stood close together – they were exactly the same size.

Just then, the farmer drove into the field. He was pulling the smallest horsebox that Mr Maggs had ever seen.

"I'm going to the Village Show today," said the little Shetland pony, "and that's my very own horsebox."

Mr Maggs thought for a moment. "That's it, Monty!" he cried. "I'll buy you one of those and we'll have great trips to the country." And he gave Monty and the Shetland pony a handful of chocolate biscuits.

So if you happen to see a rather small horsebox driving along, take a close look, it could be Mr Maggs and Monty!

He's Behind You!

Every time Baby Bear and Father Bear went walking through the forest where they lived, they would play a special game. It was Baby Bear's favourite. Each time they went out together, Father Bear would walk in front with Baby Bear a little way behind…and this is how the game was played.

As Father Bear went along, Baby Bear would creep up at the back of him and shout in his loudest voice, "HE'S BEHIND YOU!"

Most of the time Father would take no notice, but every so often, he would spin round and grab Baby Bear if he could catch him.

It was such fun. Father Bear enjoyed it as much as Baby Bear.

As they walked through the trees, Father Bear would pretend to pick flowers or talk to one of his forest friends, while Baby Bear crept up behind him.

Watch Father Bear let Baby Bear get up very close and shout, "HE'S BEHIND YOU!"

This time he's caught him!
And this time he's missed!
One afternoon Father and Baby
Bear had been down by the lake on
the very edge of the forest.
"HE'S BEHIND YOU!"

laughed Baby Bear, slowly creeping
up on Father Bear as they headed for
the trees.
But what is this?
HE'S NOT BEHIND YOU!
HE'S IN FRONT OF YOU!

Sam Spider's New Shoes

"I need new shoes," said Sam Spider one day.

"But you never wear shoes, you silly spider!" snapped a big shiny beetle.

"I know," sighed Sam, "that's why my socks are always full of holes!"

So off Sam scurried to the shoe shop. His friends went along to give him some advice.

Soon Sam Spider had looked in all the shoe boxes. "There are so many," he said, "I simply can't choose!"

"With your legs," whispered the dainty dragonfly, "you should wear ballet shoes or satin slippers."

"With your legs," muttered the big shiny beetle, "I think you should wear football boots!"

"Don't forget the wet weather," added the slug. "A good pair of Wellingtons would come in handy!"

"It's no good!" Sam cried. "I still can't decide, so I'll take them all."

"There's just one thing I want to know," called the big shiny beetle as he marched away. "What on earth are you going to do with all those shoe boxes?"

Cookie Dolls

The children baked a batch of cookies and left them on the kitchen table overnight.

When the family had gone to bed, the Wooden Spoon People came out of their drawer to take a look around the kitchen.

"You're all very plain!" said one of the wooden spoons, as he stared hard at the cookies.

"You would look plain too if you only had two currants for eyes and half a cherry for a nose," sighed a cookie quite sadly.

"So sorry," the wooden spoon apologized. "I didn't mean to sound so rude."

And with that, he leapt back into the kitchen drawer, and rummaged around until he found what he was looking for.

"May I introduce you to my friend the icing pump?" asked the wooden spoon, as the two came over to the astonished cookies. "He's the fellow you need!"

In no time at all, the wooden spoons grabbed mixing bowls and icing sugar and all kinds of pretty decorations.

The icing pump got busy and made every different pattern he could think of, with icing in all colours of the rainbow.

"We all look so beautiful," smiled a cookie who was covered in every shade of pink. "We look good enough to eat!"

Miss Mole Catches a Ghost

Quite often Miss Mole would look after the young ones who lived in the woodland, when their parents went out in the evening.

"I just love baby-sitting," sighed Miss Mole, as she gazed at the little animals, "you're all such darlings!"

"But we're not babies," grumbled the fieldmice twins, "we're almost grown up!"

"Well, you'll always be babies to me," giggled Miss Mole, as she

gave them all a great big hug.

But one evening when Miss Mole was baby-sitting, something very strange happened…

All the little animals had walked over to Miss Mole's house just before dark. They were laughing and joking and making lots of noise as they went along.

All of a sudden one of the rabbits heard a strange sound. Then one or two of the little animals saw something move near the top of the trees.

"What was that?" gasped a baby badger as he grabbed one of the squirrels.

Then, as the wind rustled the leaves on the tree…they all saw it…a spooky white thing flying through the branches!

"It's a ghost!" screamed a small hedgehog. And everyone ran as fast as they could and landed in a heap at Miss Mole's front door.

"Whatever is wrong?" cried

Miss Mole as she opened her door, and in fell all the little animals.

"We've seen a ghost!" sobbed the rabbit. "It's chased us all the way through the wood, and now it's up in that tree!"

Miss Mole put on her extra strong glasses and took a good look.

"Goodness me," she gasped, "there it is!"

Right then and there, brave Miss Mole reached for her longest broom and pulled something out of the branches above.

"Here's your ghost," laughed Miss Mole. "It's a plastic bag. I lost it on my way back from the woodland supermarket!"

All the little animals breathed a big sigh of relief as Miss Mole took them inside and closed the door.

"Gather round and I'll tell you a story," she said kindly.

"As long as it's not a ghost story," whispered the baby badger.

The Three Bears' Pyjamas

One morning in the early post there was a parcel for each of the three bears.

The three parcels were exactly the same shape and size. Inside were three pairs of brand new pyjamas, exactly the same shape and size, which was lucky…because the three bears were exactly the same shape and size too!

"How lovely to get brand new pyjamas!" cried one of the bears as he looked down at the ones he was wearing. "Our pyjamas are far too small and almost worn out!"

Now the three bears had a problem – which pair to choose.

"I can't decide," said the first bear.

"I like them all," said the second bear.

"I want the red top from one pair and the yellow bottoms from another!" said the third, as he looked inside all three boxes.

Then Mrs Bear began to laugh. "I think I've solved your problem. Mix and match your new pyjamas!"

"You mean muddle them up," chuckled the three bears…and that's exactly what they did.

The Happy Tappers

Dolly, Molly and Holly were three little sisters who liked swimming and dancing and all kinds of sport.

They went to gymnastics on Monday, ballet on Tuesday, judo on Thursday and ice-skating on Friday.

"Sometimes I feel like a taxi service!" said Dad, as he drove them home one evening. "At least Wednesday night is free."

"Not any more!" Mum smiled. "Dolly, Molly and Holly are starting tap-dancing classes on Wednesday."

At the end of the first lesson, the tap-dancing teacher said, "Dolly, Molly and Holly, I want you to go home and practise, practise, practise!"

Now these three little girls didn't need to be told to practise, in fact once they put on their tap shoes, they couldn't stop dancing. They tapped in the kitchen, they tapped in the hall, they tapped up the stairs and across the bedroom floor.

"Whatever will our next door neighbour Mr Bell say, when he hears all that tapping?" asked Dad. But he needn't have worried.

"When your girls are happily tapping," said Mr Bell, "I shall play the organ very loudly, then I shall strum on my banjo."

"And I shall take the dog out for a very long walk!" sighed Dad.

31

Bathtime at the Zoo

All the animals at the zoo loved bathtime, especially the little ones, because it was so much fun.

Norah, the zoo-keeper's wife, made quite sure the water was not too hot nor too cold, while the zoo-keeper fetched enough dry towels for everyone – even the giraffes!

Now one summer evening, just before supper, Norah called the animals together before bathtime. As soon as everything was ready, the baby monkey climbed up on Norah's knee and whispered in her ear.

"I would like a banana sandwich and a chocolate milk shake for supper," he whispered in a tiny voice.

"Then I shall make them for you straight after bathtime," smiled Norah, and she gave him a hug and a kiss.

"I would like you to read me the story about Snow White," the baby monkey whispered softly.

"Then I shall read it to you straight after you've had your bath," said Norah, as she lifted

the baby monkey off her knee and reached for the soap.

"I don't want to have a bath," the baby monkey yelled at the top of his voice, "and I'm not going to have a bath again, never ever!" and he stamped his tiny feet.

"Oh dear!" the zoo-keeper sighed. "I think we have a problem," and he went off to fetch more towels.

So Norah and the rest of the animals did their best to show the baby monkey what fun he could have in the water.

But it was no use! Very soon everyone was soaking wet – all

except the baby monkey, who had managed to keep absolutely dry.

When the zoo-keeper came back with some more dry towels and found everyone soaking wet, he began to laugh. Then he reached deep into his jacket pocket.

He bent down to the baby monkey and whispered to him, "I brought this just for you from the zoo shop." And into his hand he popped a tiny toy monkey that bobbed up and down in water.

"He looks just like me," giggled the baby monkey, and he jumped into the bath straightaway.

"What a relief!" said Norah, as she went off to get dried and make the animals' supper.

Patsy's Playpen

Patsy's baby brother could be quite a nuisance, especially when the little girl was trying to knit or sew.

"He won't leave my pins and needles alone," grumbled Patsy, "and he's always after my sharp scissors!"

One day the little girl had a brilliant idea.

Now Patsy's little brother always screamed loudly whenever he was put into his playpen. He hated being inside it.

"I'll hop in there and do my sewing," giggled Patsy, "then we shall all have some peace!"

35

Who's Afraid of the Dark?

The Little Blue Monkey was afraid of the dark. Each night when all the toys went to bed, everything was fine until Teddy switched off the light.

"There's nothing to be afraid of in the dark," whispered the doll kindly when the Little Blue Monkey kept getting out of bed.

"But I'm frightened and I want the light back on!" yelled the Little Blue Monkey at the top of his voice.

"Oh dear!" said Teddy. "It looks as if we shall be awake all night."

So he got out of bed and searched through all the cupboards and drawers until he found what he was looking for.

"Here you are," said Teddy, and he gave the Little Blue Monkey a splendid torch.

The tiny monkey was happy at last. The light was switched off and everyone fell fast asleep...but not the Little Blue Monkey.

He shone his new torch round and round the room; he shone it under the beds and in the toys' faces.

"Perhaps the torch wasn't such a good idea after all," said Teddy, yawning.

So the very next day Teddy went out and bought the little monkey his very own night-light, and the problem was solved.

The toys got some sleep and the Little Blue Monkey left his tiny light on all night long.

Kitty Pumpkin

Megan's little puppies were born at Christmas time, so she had no trouble at all thinking of names for them.

"I think I shall call one Cracker," said Megan.

"How about calling the other Jingle?" suggested her mum.

"Why don't you call them Christmas and Cracker?" giggled Megan's brother, who was always being silly.

In the end Megan called her two little puppies Snowball and Snowflake, which everyone agreed was just perfect.

Now the next Hallowe'en, Grandpa Joe brought Megan her very own kitten.

"What shall I call you?" whispered Megan as she held her kitten closely.

"How about Spooky or Broomstick?" asked her brother, silly as ever.

"Her fur is golden and she has pale yellow eyes," whispered Grandpa Joe. "You could call her Pumpkin."

"That's perfect, Grandpa Joe," cried Megan. "My very own kitten who came on Hallowe'en. I shall call her Kitty Pumpkin!"

The Bubble Gum Boat

Iggy Frog promised that he would look after all his little nephews and nieces for an afternoon.

Now Iggy Frog was very lazy, and when all the little frogs arrived, he pretended to be fast asleep on his boat.

"Wake up Uncle Iggy!" one of the tiny frogs yelled in Iggy's ear.

"I want you all to keep very quiet this afternoon," said Iggy, slowly opening his eyes. "No talking, no shouting and definitely no croaking!" And with that, he made himself comfortable and went to sleep.

So the little frogs, who always did as they were told, went off to play without making a sound.

"How very peaceful and quiet," murmured Iggy as he snoozed in the sun. "Just perfect!"

Then all of a sudden, something went 'POP'!

Iggy opened his eyes, then 'POP', there it was again.

'POP, POP, POP'! The noise was deafening. 'POP, POP, POP'!

Can you believe it? Every little frog had brought along a whole packet of bubble gum. 'POP, POP, POP'! all round poor Iggy.

"Stop that noise!" yelled Iggy, but the little frogs were too busy 'popping' to hear.

Just then, a broken branch came floating by on the river. It bumped into Iggy's boat and made two big holes in the side. At once water poured in and poor Iggy's boat began to sink.

When the little frogs saw their Uncle Iggy trying his best to save the boat, they stopped blowing bubbles immediately and rushed over to help.

Quick as they could, the little frogs stuck their bubble gum over the holes. The water stopped pouring in at once and Iggy's boat was saved.

"Can we make a noise now?" the little frogs chorused.

"Yes!" sighed Iggy. "You can make as much noise as you like. I won't get any more sleep this afternoon, I shall be mending my boat!"

Hoot and Snowy Save the Lifeboat

The lifeboat crew had been very busy all morning getting their boat ready to put to sea – if there was an emergency.

But the weather was very calm and no-one seemed to need rescuing at all.

"This afternoon, if everything is still quiet, we shall put to sea and pretend there is an emergency," the Captain told Snowy the Seagull, who always went out with the lifeboat.

So that afternoon, when everything was ready, the lifeboat was launched and was soon far out to sea. Then suddenly, without any warning, the engines stopped and all was quiet.

"Whatever is wrong?" asked Snowy the Seagull, as the Captain poked his head out of the engine room.

"I'm afraid we've run out of fuel," said the Captain, his face turning bright red, "and we've forgotten to bring some spare fuel on board with us!"

By now the lifeboat had drifted far out to sea. The Captain and his crew looked very glum, and no-one seemed to know what to do.

But suddenly Snowy the Seagull heard a familiar sound. He perched on top of the mast and looked around. Then he flapped his wings and flew swiftly across the waves.

Now Snowy had heard the "Toot, toot, toot," of his friend Hoot the Tug far away over the sea.

When at last he reached the tug, the seagull flew down and perched on Hoot's funnel, and very soon the tug was chugging across the waves towards the lifeboat.

"Glad to see you, Hoot!" cried the Captain as he threw a towing line across. "Snowy, you're a hero!"

So Hoot towed the lifeboat back into harbour and everyone returned safe and sound.

"No need to tell everyone we ran out of fuel," whispered the Captain to Snowy, "can we pretend it was just an exercise?"

"Your secret is safe with me…and Hoot!" called Snowy the Seagull as he flew off.

Baby Hedgehog and the Yellow Butterfly

It was a lovely day and all the little hedgehogs were playing tennis. All, that is, except Baby Hedgehog. He was sitting on the grass looking very bored.

"Why can't I play tennis too?" he asked, as he watched his brothers and sisters having a really good game.

"Because you're far too small!" said his biggest brother, kindly. "The tennis ball could hit you on the nose and that would hurt a little chap like you," and he went back to play with the others.

So Baby Hedgehog looked around for something to do.

Just then a bright yellow butterfly fluttered by. Straightaway Baby Hedgehog jumped up and began to chase it.

The yellow butterfly flew through the meadow, over the bridge across the stream, and on towards the edge of the dark wood.

Now when the yellow butterfly went deeper and deeper into the dark wood, the little hedgehog followed, scurrying behind as fast as his short legs would go.

At last the yellow butterfly settled on a flower, and Baby Hedgehog sat down, quite out of breath. As he looked around, the little hedgehog found that he was lost, and he began to cry.

"I'll never find my way back," he sobbed very loudly, "and I want to go home to my mum!"

43

When the yellow butterfly realized what had happened she started to fly back through the trees.

"Follow me!" she called to the little hedgehog. But very soon she stopped. "My wings are too tired to fly any farther," she said, "but my friend the woodpecker will take you to the edge of the dark wood."

So Baby Hedgehog followed the woodpecker.

At the edge of the dark wood the woodpecker stopped. "This is as far as I go," he said, "but my friend the robin will take you all the way to the stream."

So Baby Hedgehog followed the robin.

"Watch!" said the robin, as he blew on a thistle. "Follow the seeds over the bridge to the other side."

Across the stream a baby hare

was waiting. "Let's run through the meadow together," said the baby hare.

So Baby Hedgehog hurried along because he could feel he was almost home.

By now darkness was falling. At the edge of the meadow two silvery moths fluttered down from the long grass.

"Follow us!" they called. And before he knew it, Baby Hedgehog had scampered across the grass and stopped at his own front door.

The other young hedgehogs were very relieved to see their little brother back home safely.

"Can I play tennis with you tomorrow?" asked Baby Hedgehog.

"Every day from now on!" they cried. And they all gave him a great big hug…as far as their prickles would allow!

The Little Knitted Pig

"I feel like going out this morning," said the Little Knitted Pig.

"It's been raining all night," said the Panda, "so you'll have to stay indoors like the rest of us."

"Look, the rain has stopped!" cried the Little Knitted Pig. "The front door is opening and they are taking the baby out."

Now the Little Knitted Pig was always popped into the pram to keep the baby quiet. This meant that he went outside almost every day.

So the Little Knitted Pig settled himself down in the pram. He was just dozing off under a soft warm blanket, when a little chubby hand grabbed hold of him and tossed him out of the pram into a very muddy puddle below!

Luckily for the Little Knitted Pig, someone noticed and picked him up dripping wet and dirty.

"Just look at the state of me!" muttered the Little Knitted Pig to himself. He was in such a mess, he had to be dropped into a plastic bag and left with the shopping at the bottom of the pram.

46

As soon as he got home, the Little Knitted Pig was tossed into the washing machine, then hung outside on the clothesline to dry.

The afternoon was sunny and warm, and very soon the Little Knitted Pig was pretty and pink and fluffy once more.

But goodness me, when he joined the other toys, he was in for a shock.

"Whatever has happened?" cried the Panda, when he saw the Little Knitted Pig. "Take a look in the mirror!"

"That can't be me!" snapped the Little Knitted Pig when he saw his reflection. "I'm not long and thin, and my ears are the wrong shape!"

So the Little Knitted Pig nodded his head, then wrinkled up his nose and flapped both ears. "You're right, it is me!" he gasped in amazement. "I must have been pulled out of shape in the washing machine."

…Now this sad story has a happy ending…

The lady who knitted our little pig came to baby-sit that very night. And when she saw the state of poor Little Knitted Pig, she unravelled all the woolly pieces…as ladies who knit do…then she cleverly knitted them back together again.

These days the Little Knitted Pig tries very hard to keep out of muddy puddles!

Climbing Frame Rescue

"How exciting it would be if we could play on the children's climbing frame in the garden," said Dolly, as she gazed out of the window.

"I wouldn't dare!" gasped the Rag Doll.

"It's far too high and very dangerous," said the Curly-haired Doll, sternly. Then she began to giggle. "But I will if you will!"

So when no-one was looking, the three dolls tiptoed out of the house and ran across the lawn until they reached the climbing frame.

"It's much bigger than I thought," said the Rag Doll, quietly.

"Nonsense!" shouted Dolly. "Race you to the top!"

It took simply ages for the three dolls to scramble up the steep climbing frame. Dolly was the first to reach the top, but when she looked down she suddenly began to feel quite frightened.

"I wish I'd never come up here," she screamed. "I want to get down at once!" and she began to cry.

Then Rag Doll, who was braver than she thought, walked carefully across the ladder to comfort poor little Dolly.

Then the Curly-haired Doll, who was trying very hard to keep her balance, took the bright red ribbon out of her hair and waved it from side to side.

"Help! Help!" the dollies shouted as loudly as they could.

Lucky for them the rest of the toys were watching from the window. And in no time at all, the toy helicopter and the plane took off to rescue the frightened dollies.

"Could the toy fire brigade please stand by in case they are needed," ordered Teddy, very grandly. "I do hope these silly dolls have learned their lesson!"

At last the three dolls were back inside, safe and sound.

"Wasn't that exciting?" said Rag Doll and Curly-haired Doll, both out of breath.

But Dolly did not answer. She'd had quite enough climbing for one day!

Mr Tappit's Giant Toy

Mr Tappit had been making toys for more than fifty years. Children loved to visit his shop and look at the shelves full of toys. Everyone was very fond of old Mr Tappit – especially all his toys, who loved him dearly.

After his work was done and the toyshop was closed, they would play games and have fun together. Quite often the toys and Mr Tappit had the most wonderful parties, and sometimes they went on picnics – if the weather was fine.

One day Mr Tappit sat in the corner of his shop, quietly thinking to himself.

"What is it?" asked the clown-doll. "Do you have a problem?"

"Not at all," smiled Mr Tappit. "I've had a bright idea. I am going to build the biggest toy I have ever made, and I want you toys to help me!"

The toys couldn't wait to get started. Early next morning they gathered all the tools while Mr Tappit measured the pieces of wood, then marked them with his pencil.

"This toy will be the biggest ever seen," cried Mr Tappit, as he ran round the shop looking for his glue pot. "In fact, it will be a GIANT!'

"Of course not," smiled Mr Tappit. "It's just a Giant Toy!"

It took a whole week, but at last the Giant Toy was finished.

"You've all worked very hard," said Mr Tappit with a smile, and he stepped back to take a look.

"Not a real giant, I hope," whispered a little doll in a shaky voice. "I'm really frightened of giants."

All the toys put down their paint pots and brushes and stepped back too.

"Isn't it wonderful!" they cried,

and everyone clapped and cheered.

The Giant Toy was a great success. After Mr Tappit had gazed for a while at the wonderful toy he had made, he heaved a sigh and scratched his head.

"Whatever am I going to do with it?" Mr Tappit asked.

The toys looked puzzled. They didn't know either. The Giant Toy was far too big to stay in the shop, and no house was large enough for a toy that size.

"I've got it!" yelled Mr Tappit, jumping into the air with glee.

"I'll put it outside my shop door. Then passers-by will see the Giant Toy and come and take a look inside at all the other toys!"

53

Mr Magic Goes Fishing

Mr Magic had a pet rabbit called Snowdrop, who helped him with his magic tricks on stage.

One day, Mr Magic said to Snowdrop, "We have given so many magic shows this year, I think we both deserve a holiday."

"What a great idea!" cried Snowdrop, who wanted to go away and have lots of fun.

"That's settled then," smiled Mr Magic. "We'll go fishing by a quiet lake and have a nice rest."

"That doesn't sound very exciting," Snowdrop thought to himself, but he said he would go, because he knew Mr Magic would enjoy it.

So Mr Magic packed his fishing rod and Snowdrop packed the magic wand (just in case they needed it), and off they went.

The weather was warm and the lake was peaceful. Mr Magic got out his rod and line and sat quietly waiting for the fish to bite. All of a sudden Mr Magic caught something …but it wasn't a fish…it was a bicycle wheel! On and on went Mr Magic pulling all kinds of rubbish out of the lake.

"It's just like our magic show!" laughed Snowdrop.

Then the little rabbit remembered the magic wand. "I think I'll try my luck," he giggled, as he waved the wand over the water.

Can you believe what Snowdrop pulled out of the lake? Even the fish got a surprise.

"This holiday is turning out to be great fun," chuckled Snowdrop. "IT'S MAGIC!"

Dancing Stars

When day is done and darkness falls, it is time for all the little insects and teeny creepy crawlies to go to sleep.

"We're not in the least bit tired!" the little ants called to one another.

"Neither are we!" the tiny fuzzy wuzzy caterpillars replied.

"We're all still wide awake!" giggled lots of little ladybirds.

"So are we!" chirped the young crickets as they jumped up and down.

"I do wish all these little insects and teeny creepy crawlies would settle down," said Bella Butterfly with a sigh. "I've been flying around the garden all day and I'm quite exhausted."

"Aren't we all, Bella?" snapped a rather grumpy beetle.

"Close your eyes and start counting sheep, you're bound to fall fast asleep," a plump old bumble bee told all the insects and teeny creepy crawlies.

This made them laugh so much, they felt more wide awake than before.

"How about counting stars instead of sheep?" suggested Bella Butterfly, yawning. "Then we can all get some sleep!"

So all the little insects and creepy crawlies looked up into the starry sky.

"We can't count the stars, they won't keep still!" they shouted, and the insects and teeny creepy crawlies stared in amazement.

"They're not stars," groaned the plump old bumble bee, "they're FIREFLIES that dance and flit and fly around all night long!"

"Just like us!" shrieked the little insects and teeny creepy crawlies in delight. "Let's party!"

"GOODNIGHT!" groaned the grown-up insects, and they all went to bed.

Fun Afternoon

It was 'Fun Afternoon' at the swimming pool. On this special day, just for fun, everyone could bring along their blow-up toys and dinghies and have a really good time.

All the children liked 'Fun Afternoon' because there was so much splashing and lots of noise!

But on one 'Fun Afternoon', everybody brought so many toys… there was no room left for the children!

Ferdy the Fire Engine

Ferdy was the smallest fire engine at the station. He came in very handy at times, because he could get down the narrowest street and into the tiniest space if there was a fire.

But often, when there was a very big fire, poor Ferdy was left at the station while the larger engines went out to fight the blaze.

"It's not fair," muttered Ferdy one day, when he had been left behind, "I'm just as useful as they are!" And he felt very sad and disappointed.

But wait…just at that moment, the lady who cooked for the firemen came dashing out of the kitchen shouting at the top of her voice.

"My frying pan is on fire! Help, Ferdy, help! You must save my kitchen!"

Fire engine Ferdy was there at once. Quick as a flash, he put out the fire. The frying pan was ruined, but the firemen's supper was saved.

"If you hadn't stayed behind, the whole fire station could have burned down," said the fire chief. "We are all very grateful to you, Ferdy!"

"Then I am useful after all," smiled Ferdy, happily.

"You're a hero, that's what you are!" chorused the firemen, as they tucked into their supper.

Sukie's New Puppy

Sukie called her new puppy Mischief, I expect you know why. From the very first day he arrived, Sukie's little dog kept getting into all kinds of mischief – which is exactly what puppies do!

"At least Mischief is quiet at night," smiled Sukie, as she popped him into his new bed.

"You can't get into any mischief in here," and she gave him a goodnight hug.

But when Sukie went upstairs to bed, she couldn't find her slippers.

"I expect Mischief has hidden them somewhere," laughed Sukie's mum. "We'll look for them tomorrow."

So Sukie brushed her teeth and combed her hair and got into bed. Looking after Mischief made her feel very tired.

"I don't usually comb my hair," murmured the little girl as she began to fall asleep, "I always brush it."

During the night everybody in the house was woken up by a strange howling noise.

"It must be Mischief!" cried Sukie, so she jumped out of bed and ran downstairs.

"What is the matter?" asked Sukie gently, as she put both arms around her puppy.

"This is the matter," laughed her dad. "Mischief is sitting on your prickly hairbrush!"

"So that's where it went," chuckled Sukie. "Tomorrow you can show me where my slippers are. Goodnight you naughty Mischief!"

Ashley Juggles Jellies

Ashley's grandma was having some of her best friends to tea.

"I would like you to come and join us," Grandma smiled sweetly, as she patted Ashley's head.

"Well I…er hum…," mumbled Ashley as he tried to think of an excuse.

"That's settled then!" said his grandma. "Be here by four o'clock sharp…there'll be lots to eat."

Now when Ashley's mum and dad heard that he was going to tea with grandma's best friends, they both began to look worried.

"Do try to behave," said Mum, as she tidied Ashley's hair.

"And please don't make a mess," said Dad, looking very anxious.

At four o'clock on the dot, when Ashley opened his grandma's front door, all her best friends were sitting down at the tea table.

"Before we have tea," Ashley's grandma announced, "a lady is coming to give us a talk on gardening."

All of a sudden the telephone rang, and when Grandma answered it, she let out a little scream.

"I'm afraid we won't be able to have our talk this afternoon, unfortunately the poor lady has had some kind of accident with a runaway wheelbarrow!"

Then Grandma looked at Ashley. "Whatever shall I do?" she asked.

"Don't worry yourself one little bit," said Ashley. "I shall take the lady's place."

"Do you know a lot about gardening?" his grandma asked in surprise.

"Nope!" replied Ashley. "But I do know everything about juggling…and I will be delighted to entertain you all before tea!"

"How lovely," smiled Grandma, and she told her guests straightaway.

So Ashley got up from the table and began to juggle.

At first he threw plates up into the air, then cups and saucers and spoons. Then he went on to sticky buns and cream cakes…and last of all…he juggled with jellies.

"Wonderful, Ashley! Bravo!" cried Grandma, and she clapped and clapped. "He hasn't got a bit of mess on my best tablecloth."

And Ashley, very proud of himself…took a bow!

The Book End Bunnies

At one end of the bookcase in the children's room was a Little Wooden Bunny.

"It's so lonely up here," he said to himself every single day. "I've no friends, no-one to talk to, and I've read every book on the book shelf at least ten times!"

The poor Little Wooden Bunny looked very glum...until one day, everything changed, as you will see...

The children's mother asked them to tidy all their books and dust the shelves. As you can imagine, it took ages.

They lifted all the books off the shelves, put them in piles all over the floor, then ran out to play. The Little Wooden Bunny was left alone on the book shelf – with not even the books for company. He couldn't help but sigh as he gazed around at the empty space.

Can you believe it? The book shelf wasn't empty at all!

Right at the other end was a wooden bunny who looked exactly the same as him.

"Have you been standing at the end of the shelf all this time?" asked the Little Wooden Bunny, very excited.

"I certainly have!" said the other wooden bunny, "and it's been so lonely."

"Not any more," laughed the Little Wooden Bunny. "From now on we'll meet every day and be the very best of friends!"

Best Friend Bracelets

Late one night a new family moved into the house next door. Rosie-Anne spotted the removal van from her bedroom window.

"I do hope they have a little girl like me," she whispered to her teddy bear. "It would be really nice to have a best friend."

So next morning, straight after breakfast, Rosie-Anne went next door and rang the bell. A big boy opened the door, and when Rosie-Anne looked up at him, she forgot what she was going to say.

"I expect you've come to see my little sis!" said the big boy. Still Rosie-Anne didn't say a word.

Then a little girl, just the same size as Rosie-Anne, peeped round the kitchen door. The two small girls looked at each other and smiled…but neither of them said a word.

The little girl took Rosie-Anne to look inside a very special box she was unpacking on the table. In the box were all kinds of braids and beads and pretty coloured threads. In no time at all, the little girl had plaited Rosie-Anne a necklace and a bracelet.

At last the little girl spoke, "I hope that you'll be my best friend."

"For ever!" said Rosie-Anne, and she giggled as she held up her new friendship bracelet.

Teddy in a Tie

Sarah's daddy often had to go away to work. Sometimes he was gone for just a few days, but every so often he had to stay away from home for a whole month.

Poor Sarah didn't like this one little bit, because she always missed her daddy a lot. Once, when he returned from one of his trips, he brought Sarah a wonderful teddy bear. Teddy became Sarah's favourite toy. The little girl took him everywhere and never let him out of her sight.

Now when Sarah's daddy went away, he would always say to her big brother, "Look after Mum and Sarah for me."

"Who shall I look after for you?" Sarah asked her daddy before he left.

"Look after Teddy for me," smiled Daddy.

"Who can Teddy look after for you?" asked Sarah.

"He can look after you and my best tie!" said Daddy, which made everyone laugh.

Cat in a Basket

In a lighthouse far out to sea lived Les, the lighthouse-keeper, and Tibby, his cat. All year round they lived in a cosy room near the top of the lighthouse. For Les and his cat Tibby had to make quite sure that the light shone brightly across the sea all the time, and never ever went out!

Tibby and Les were never lonely, they had each other for company, and they both liked that. Once a week a boat came over from the mainland to deliver letters and parcels. The crew always brought a big basket of groceries for Les, and lots of tins of tuna for Tibby – because tuna was his favourite!

Sometimes when the sea was very rough, the boat couldn't tie up to the rocks. Then the crew didn't visit the lighthouse that week. Instead Les and Tibby hauled the basketful of groceries on a rope up to the top window. They took out all their groceries, then sent the empty basket back down on the rope to the waiting boat.

"Would you like to go back in the basket sometimes?" Les asked Tibby. "Then you could go over to the mainland for a week's holiday."

But Tibby just shook his head, jumped up onto the lighthouse-keeper's knee, purred very loudly and settled down for a long nap.

Now every single day there was another welcome visitor to the lighthouse. It was Snowy Seagull. He would fly up to the top of the lighthouse and tap on the window to be let in.

Now Snowy usually called mid-morning when Les was making his coffee and opening the biscuit tin.

"It's a lovely day out there," said Snowy, as he enjoyed a ginger biscuit. "Have you been down onto the rocks this morning, Tibby?"

Tibby shook his head. "It's such a long way down. There are three hundred and sixty-five steps – one for every day of the year," the little cat went on, "I don't mind running all the way down, but it's an awful long way back up again."

"Pity you don't know how to fly!" joked Snowy.

"It is a shame," said Les with a grin, but he knew how much Tibby liked to go down onto the rocks to chase crabs – just little ones, of course!

Now as Les put away the biscuit tin, he glanced at his cupboard full of groceries, and it gave him a brilliant idea.

"CAT IN A BASKET!" he shouted at the top of his voice. "We'll put Tibby in a basket and lower him down the side of the lighthouse!"

"I can fly along with Tibby and make sure that he is safe," said Snowy.

So that is what they did.

Now Tibby really is a 'cat in a basket'. He plays on the rocks for as long as he likes, and when he is ready to go back to the top of the lighthouse, he hops into the basket, gives a tug on the rope, and Les hauls Tibby back to the top again.

The Undersea Show

The creatures who lived near the sunken treasure ship, deep down at the bottom of the ocean, were feeling rather glum.

"Whatever is the matter?" asked a jolly jellyfish as he floated past. "Do cheer up!"

"We're so bored," sighed a fish pulling a face and pouting, which sent trails of bubbles up to the surface.

"How can you be bored?" asked the jellyfish, very surprised. "You have a whole sunken treasure ship to explore."

"We've explored it hundreds of times," sighed the fish once again, making more bubbles.

"And we're tired of playing pirates and finding chests full of treasure – so don't suggest it!" snapped a grumpy catfish.

"Sorry!" said the jellyfish. "Just trying to help," and he floated off to talk to a starfish he knew well.

So the rest of that morning, the fish deep down at the bottom of the ocean swam round and round looking miserable…you know the feeling, when you can't think of anything to do at all!

Then, after lunch, the jellyfish floated back, and this time he brought his friend the starfish with him.

"I have been hearing how the undersea creatures used to put on a fantastic show!" said the jellyfish.

"In those days," the starfish added, "we had a stage with curtains and scenery. Everybody sang and danced – we were all such stars!"

All the fish swam across at once, looking very interested.

"When do we start rehearsals?" chuckled the octopus, waving his arms. "I can't wait to be in a show."

"Wait a minute!" cried the sea horse. "Where's our stage?"

"Follow me to the sunken treasure ship and you will see!" shouted the starfish as he swam ahead.

As quick as could be, the undersea creatures rushed over to the old wreck and they began rehearsing straightaway. The starfish remembered all the songs and dances he used to perform, and the fish practised them again and again.

At last they were ready. 'The Undersea Show' was about to begin…

"Wait a minute!" gasped the little oysters. "The show can't go on. We have no spotlights to light up the stage." They all began to cry with disappointment.

"You're forgetting us!" shouted the electric eels as they hurried over. "We'll light up your show."

So curtain up, lights and music. 'The Undersea Show' has begun!

Gordon's Breakfast Boxes

Gordon the Gorilla loved his breakfast. He always got up in plenty of time to eat lots and lots.

"Gorillas need a big breakfast to keep them fit and strong," said Gordon, as he toasted a whole loaf of bread, then spread every slice with thick butter and plum jam.

And to finish off, Gordon drank six glasses of milk and munched a big bunch of ripe bananas.

After breakfast one morning he called to see the children who lived next door.

"What are those little boxes on the table?" asked Gordon, very interested.

"That's our breakfast cereal," said the kids. "We each choose a different box every day, and if we're feeling very hungry…we have two!"

"What a great idea," cried Gordon, "I simply love cereals!"

So the very next time Gordon went shopping, he bought all sorts of different boxes of cereal.

And from then on, he had a different box every day…and two if he felt hungry!

How Big is Jolly Monster?

"Summer's here!" cried Jolly Monster one warm bright morning. "I shall find my shorts and T-shirt and put them on today."

But, dear oh dear, Jolly Monster hadn't worn his summer clothes since last year, and they were far too small.

"I must have grown quite a bit," said Jolly Monster as he held up his shorts and T-shirt.

"Do you know the best way to measure a monster?" asked his friend.

"I don't have a tape measure or a ruler long enough," said Jolly Monster, shaking his head.

"Then come with me," his friend chuckled. "This is how to measure a monster."

So Jolly Monster and his friend carefully marked how tall they both were. And they agreed to come back in a few weeks' time to see how much they had grown.

Perhaps one day they'll reach the top!

73

Maggie's Muddy Puddle

Maggie wanted some new Wellington boots. "They must be very big and very bright red. Get me some at once!" she shouted at the top of her voice.

Now Maggie was a very demanding young lady, and when she wanted something, she always made a great fuss until she got it.

"Now I have my Wellingtons," yelled Maggie, "why isn't it raining?"

And believe it or not, at that very moment, the lightning flashed, the thunder crashed and it began to pour with rain.

Very soon the street in front of Maggie's house was full of muddy puddles...very muddy puddles indeed.

"I'm going out!" bawled Maggie, as she pulled on her new red Wellingtons then kicked the front door closed.

"My goodness," whispered her mother, "she's going to get very wet." But this was exactly what Maggie had been waiting for.

Shouting and yelling at the top of her voice, she jumped in all the muddiest puddles she could find, and splashed and soaked everyone that passed by.

...But look, coming along the street is someone who loves muddy puddles even more than Maggie!

Mrs Hedgehog's New Towels

How do you dry lots of little hedgehogs after they have just had a bath?

It's terribly difficult with all those prickles!

One night, after bathtime, poor Mrs Hedgehog gazed at her towels in dismay. Every one of them was full of holes – even the bath mat was frayed.

"Oh dear!" said Mrs Hedgehog with a sigh. "I only bought new towels last week – this will never do!"

Now the very next day, when she was looking through her magazine, she saw the answer to the problem.

So she set off at once to the shop that sold sheets, pillowcases and very soft fluffy towels. She went straight to the counter and found exactly what she wanted.

"I'll take one of those for each of my little hedgehogs, please," she said, and paid her bill.

Then Mrs Hedgehog went back home and waited until bathtime… and when each little hedgehog stepped out of the water dripping wet…she popped a new robe onto every one of them.

"These will dry you out in no time at all," laughed Mrs Hedgehog, "and my towels will stay as good as new!"

Helen Hamster was very inquisitive. "I just need to know!" she would say, as she poked her little pink nose into someone else's business.

One day Helen Hamster found a box in the garden. It was the strangest box with drawn-on windows and a painted-on door.

"There's no lid," said Helen, as she tried to find a way to open the box. "I must find out what's inside!"

So that nosy little hamster got down on the grass and tried to lift up the box to peep underneath.

"That's my box!" said a voice behind her. It was Hamish Hamster from next door.

"There's nothing inside," said Helen, rather disappointed. "It's quite empty."

"I know," said Hamish, "but it's not going to stay that way."

"What are you going to put inside your mystery box?" asked Helen, inquisitive as ever.

"Me!" said Hamish, as he turned the box the right way up.

"Do tell me. Why are you getting into an empty box?" snapped Helen, rather vexed.

"To get away from you!" replied Hamish with a big smile.

And with that, he fetched a little ladder, climbed into the box and pulled the ladder up after him.

Hiding From Helen

The Clock That Went Backwards

One night, just before bedtime, Lewis and Rusty's granddad popped in to visit for a little while.

"You almost missed us, Granddad," smiled Lewis, "we're off to bed!"

"Before you go," said Granddad, "open this present I've brought for you."

Lewis and Rusty pulled off the wrapping paper eagerly.

"What a lovely clock!" gasped Rusty. "It isn't our birthday and it definitely isn't Christmas. Is the clock ours to keep?"

"It certainly is!" replied Granddad. Then he bent down and whispered in the children's ears, "this is a very special clock. It was in my bedroom when I was a little boy. Tonight, when Mum tells you a bedtime story, look at the time on the clock and you will be in for a surprise."

At seven-thirty their mum began to read a bedtime story – it lasted fifteen minutes, but when the children looked at the new clock – it was only seven-fifteen!

"It's a magic clock," giggled Lewis very quietly, "it goes backwards!"

As it was still only seven-fifteen, the children had another story, then another and another – and their clock still kept going backwards.

Mum smiled quietly to herself…she knew the secret of the 'clock that went backwards' – because it was in her bedroom when she was a little girl!

When William went outside to play, his friend, Buzz the Robot, always went too.

"Play baseball! Play baseball!" cried Buzz in his funny robot voice.

"Just a minute!" laughed William, and he ran to get his glove and bat and ball.

Now Buzz was very good at baseball. He had just hit the ball right across the garden when it began to pour with rain.

The Rusty Robot

"Hurry inside, Buzz," yelled William, "or you'll get rusty!"

So Buzz the Robot whizzed back into the house, feeling very disappointed indeed.

"I wish you didn't have to go inside every time it rains," said William.

"Had an idea! Had an idea!" whirred Buzz, and all his lights flashed on and off.

"Hey, that's my mum's new umbrella. You can see right through it!" laughed William.

"Just perfect! Just perfect!" chattered Buzz, and he whirled back outside to the garden under the see-through umbrella.

"You can go outside to play now every time it rains, Buzz," laughed William.

"Never get rusty! Never get rusty!" and Buzz the Robot flashed his lights on and off in glee.

Kangaroo's Kite

One day a present arrived for Kangaroo. It was from his great-aunt Cassy, who just loved sending surprises in the post.

"I wonder what it can be?" Kangaroo asked.

"Look, there's a label tied to the back!" squawked Cockatoo.

'Fly high in the sky', it read. Cockatoo took off at once and flew up into the air screeching loudly.

"It doesn't mean you!" laughed Kangaroo, and he opened his present at once.

I suppose that you've already guessed what was inside…a beautiful kite with a long tail.

"How lucky," said Kangaroo, "it's a windy day so I shall fly my kite this very minute!"

The new kite flew up in the air straightaway. It went so high, Kangaroo had to let out more and more string.

"Isn't this great!" yelled Kangaroo, as he followed his kite with great long leaps and bounds.

Now this made the new kite dip and dive. Suddenly it fell towards the ground and got caught in a tree.

"Don't worry!" squawked Cockatoo, and he flew up into the tree and brought back the kite.

"You'll have to remember not to bounce up and down like a kangaroo when you're kite-flying," laughed Cockatoo.

"I am a kangaroo!" giggled Kangaroo. "But I will try to remember."

The Dolphin Rescue

The Striped Submarine always felt a bit sleepy in the afternoon.

"I think I shall slowly sink right down to the bottom of the sea and take a little nap," she said drowsily. "Drifting, dreaming, sinking slowly – I'm almost asleep already."

The Striped Submarine had nearly nodded off when she noticed a shoal of bright little fishes swimming round and round her.

"We need your help!" the little fishes cried all together. "The dolphins are having a race and they are swimming straight towards a huge steel net. Hurry, hurry, you must help us!"

The dolphins were swimming so quickly they were almost there.

Then the Striped Submarine switched on her lights and their powerful beams lit up the seabed. At the very last moment the dolphins saw the net in the Striped Submarine's lights. Swiftly they swam up to the surface, leapt high in the air above the waves, then dived down into the sea on the other side of the net.

"Thank you Striped Submarine!" the dolphins cried. "By switching on your lights, you have saved us from being caught in that dreadful net."

"Happy to help," smiled the Striped Submarine. "Now I'll get on with my afternoon nap!"

The Chocolate Train

Minnie and Winnie's Uncle Fred lived in a house by the railway line. Many years ago Uncle Fred had been a train driver, and he still loved to see and hear the trains go by.

It was Uncle Fred's birthday in a couple of days, so Minnie and Winnie went into town to look for a present for him.

Now Uncle Fred had a wonderful model railway in his spare room, so the very first place Minnie and Winnie visited was the model railway shop.

"We could buy Uncle Fred an engine or some trucks," said Winnie.

"But everything is so expensive!" sighed Minnie, as she looked inside her purse.

"Never mind," smiled Mum, "I'll buy Uncle Fred an engine, and you can give him a present he would like just as much!"

"What is it? What is it?" cried the twins together.

"Now think hard!" said Mum. "What does Uncle Fred like to eat the best?"

"Chocolate biscuits!" yelled Minnie.

"Chocolate sponge roll!" cried Winnie.

"Let's buy some straightaway," said Mum. "Then we'll go home and make something that Uncle Fred would really like!"

…And this is what Minnie and Winnie made (with a little help from Mum of course!)

So Uncle Fred got his model engine, and a very special birthday cake too!

Eggbert Takes Off

Eggbert Egg was spending the day at the seaside with his friends – who happened to be eggs too!

The eggs loved playing games on the beach, because the sand was so soft and the little waves were so gentle...and eggs have to be very careful that they don't get cracked or broken.

Now the eggs were having a wonderful day out, all except Eggbert. He was sitting on the edge of the rocks looking far out to sea.

"Do be careful!" called a little brown egg whose name was Eggbertina. "Some of those rocks are very sharp. You could slip and fall and be smashed into little pieces!"

Little Eggbertina sounded really worried.

"Nonsense!" snapped Eggbert rather rudely. "I can never do anything really exciting. I'm always being careful!"

"You can't be too careful if you're an egg," replied Eggbertina, "or you might end up like Humpty Dumpty. He had a great fall and no-one could put him back together again!"

This made Eggbert laugh.

"I'm sorry I snapped at you, Eggbertina. But I do wish that sometimes I could swing on a swing, or climb up a climbing frame and whizz down a slide," said Eggbert with a deep sigh.

"You would almost certainly fall off and be smashed," said Eggbertina in a trembly little voice, "then I would never see you again."

This made Eggbert feel very ashamed, for he knew he had frightened poor little Eggbertina.

That night, when Eggbert fell asleep in his super-soft bed, he dreamed that he was a ski-jumper

and a rock-climber and a baseball player.

But the next morning when he woke up, Eggbert felt very disappointed. "I shall never be able to do any of those exciting things, because I am an egg, and I cannot get broken!"

Then a very strange thing happened...when Eggbert picked up his newspaper, a big notice on the back page caught his eye, it read…

DO YOU EVER DREAM OF
THRILLS AND EXCITEMENT?
JOIN OUR CLUB AND YOU
COULD JUMP OFF THE
HIGHEST BRIDGE OR TALLEST
BUILDING IN COMPLETE
SAFETY!

"That's for me!" cried Eggbert,
and he rushed off to find out about it.

The other eggs began to get
quite worried when Eggbert was
missing for a whole day. No-one
knew where he was…not even
Eggbertina!

When Eggbert did at last return,
he was very excited.

"Can you all meet tomorrow
at the bottom of Deep Valley under
Sky-high Bridge?" Eggbert asked his
friends. "I'll drop in and join you
later!"

All the eggs looked very puzzled
indeed. So very early next morning
everyone met at the bottom of Deep
Valley.

"I wonder where Eggbert is?"
asked little Eggbertina.

All of a sudden she glanced up,
and there was Eggbert plunging
towards her on the end of a very
long line.

The eggs screamed with fright.

"He'll be smashed into tiny
pieces!" shrieked Eggbertina, and
she hid her eyes.

"Look at me!" yelled Eggbert.
"I'm BUNGEE-JUMPING, and I'm
safe as can be!"

Eggbert had almost reached the
ground when the springy rope pulled
him back up to the bridge.

"It's wonderful!" Eggbert
shouted down to the astonished eggs.
"You should try it sometime!"

"I think I will," giggled
Eggbertina, and she rushed off to
bungee-jump with Eggbert!

85

Dotty Has a Visitor

Dottie the dinosaur was very forgetful.

"I have a feeling that something really special is happening today, but I can't remember what it is!" said Dottie, looking puzzled.

Just then the door bell rang. When Dottie opened her front door, Poppy, the girl from the flower shop, was standing there. She was holding a big bunch of flowers and a large basket of fruit.

"Hi, Dottie!" said Poppy with a smile. "Here are the flowers and fruit you ordered to be delivered this morning."

"Did I?" Dottie asked. "I wonder why?"

Poppy shook her head...she knew how forgetful Dottie could be.

"I know I ordered flowers and fruit," giggled Dottie. "I just can't remember why!"

So Poppy went into Dottie's kitchen and made a cup of tea. Then they both sat down to try and solve the mystery.

"I know it isn't your birthday," said Poppy, as she poured the tea.

"You're quite right," replied Dottie, "it isn't my birthday and it isn't anyone's birthday that I know!"

Try as they might, Dottie and Poppy couldn't think of a single reason why the little dinosaur had ordered the flowers and fruit.

"Look at the time!" cried Poppy, as she glanced up at the clock. "It's almost eleven. I must get back to my shop!"

"Almost eleven!" Dottie gasped. "I've just remembered. My friend is arriving at the railway station in ten minutes. I'm supposed to meet her there. Whatever shall I do?"

And poor Dottie began to rush round her kitchen in a panic... "I've a cake to bake...the breakfast pots to wash...the furniture to dust...and the whole house needs vacuuming, and I only have ten minutes!"

"I'll meet your friend," suggested Poppy. "I pass the railway station on the way back to my flower shop."

"You're so helpful," cried Dottie, and she ran towards Poppy and gave her a great big dinosaur hug.

"By the way," shouted Poppy as she rushed out of Dottie's front door, "what does your friend look like?"

But Dottie had switched on the dishwasher, the food mixer and the vacuum cleaner all at once...the noise was so loud she couldn't hear a thing.

"I must hurry or I'll miss her!" Poppy yelled as she jumped into her delivery truck.

"I wonder if Dottie's friend has blonde hair or dark hair. Is she tall or is she short? And how will I recognize her?" Poppy thought to herself as she drove along. "I shall just have to wait and see!"

The train had already pulled in when Poppy reached the railway station. The passengers were gone and all the carriages were empty.

"Oh dear!" sighed Poppy.

have known that Dottie's friend would be another dinosaur!"

So Poppy took the Little Yellow Dinosaur home on the back of her delivery truck (she was a bit too big to sit inside).

"I came all the way here with the driver in his engine," the Little Yellow Dinosaur told Dottie when

"I must have missed her."

All of a sudden, the driver stepped down from his engine at the front of the train, and with him was… A LITTLE YELLOW DINOSAUR!

Poppy began to laugh. "I should

they met. "The carriages were too small for me, and the driver said he had never had a dinosaur aboard his train before!"

"I can quite believe that!" said Poppy, as she waved goodbye and drove back to the flower shop.

Treasure Hunt Muddle

It was the beginning of the school holidays and all the note pads, pens and pencils had been shut up in the school bag.

"It's going to be really boring if we have to stay in here for a few weeks," grumbled one of the pencils.

"Then let's open the bag, jump out and find something to do," suggested a small notebook.

"Good idea!" said the pencil sharpener. "We could pretend that we are back at school."

"Oh no!" yelled the pencils. "Let's do something really exciting for once!"

But however hard they tried, not one of the pens or pencils could think of a thing.

"I went on a treasure hunt once," said a blue envelope.

"That's it!" cried the green eraser. "We'll have our very own treasure hunt!"

"I'll run ahead and mark all the clues with black crosses," shouted the ballpoint pen. "The rest of you turn around, close your eyes and count to one hundred!"

But one little red pencil didn't close his eyes at all or count to one hundred. For he wanted to help with the treasure hunt too.

"I'm such a bright red colour," whispered the little pencil, "I'm just perfect for drawing the arrows that lead to the treasure!"

So while everybody else was counting up to one hundred, the little red pencil started work.

The others were still counting…ninety-seven, ninety-eight, ninety-nine, one hundred! At last they opened their eyes and the hunt began.

The pencils and pens, the erasers and the note pads all rushed around in every direction. A few of them followed green dots and blue arrows; others looked out for black crosses. Everyone else followed lots of bright red arrows pointing all over the place. After a while everyone ended up in one big muddle!

"We're all going round in circles!" snapped the blue pencils.

"Because everyone has followed the red arrows," yelled the green pencil, very angry. "Where did they come from?"

"I drew them all," whispered the little red pencil, "I thought I was helping," and he began to cry.

Everyone felt rather ashamed when they saw the poor little red pencil in tears.

"Don't cry, little fellow. It's just a game!" smiled the green eraser, kindly. "I'll rub out all the marks in next to no time. Then we'll begin again!"

So it was agreed that this time everyone closed their eyes and counted up to one hundred…and can you guess who they asked to mark out clues? The bright little red pencil, of course!

Ma Bramley's New Car

Ma and Pa Bramley lived in the country with their little pet pig, Pippin. Now Ma and Pa Bramley had an orchard, and Pippin would often stroll through the trees and munch an apple or two.

"I like green apples the best," Pippin told Ma Bramley one day. "They're crisp and juicy and such a pretty colour."

"That may be so," said Ma Bramley, looking down at Pippin, "but I think you've had quite enough shiny green apples for such a little pig!"

And Ma Bramley gave Pippin a great big hug because she was so fond of her little pet pig.

"Come to town with me and we'll go shopping," said Ma, as she lifted Pippin into Pa's old truck.

Now Ma Bramley and Pippin had almost reached town when the truck broke down.

"I'm afraid it won't start, Pippin!" said Ma as she lifted up the bonnet. "We'll have to walk the rest of the way."

As they strolled down the High Street, Ma Bramley and Pippin passed a car showroom and Ma happened to glance inside.

"Look, Pippin, look!" gasped Ma, as she pointed to a beautiful little car next to the window.

"It reminds me of the shiny green apples in our orchard," chuckled Pippin.

But when the little pig turned around, Ma Bramley was already in

the showroom sitting in the shiny apple green car.

"It's the car of my dreams!" sighed Ma, as she lifted Pippin onto the front seat beside her.

Then she gave the salesman lots of money and drove back home as quick as she could to show Pa.

"Now that's a colour!" Pa said with a grin when he saw Ma's new car. "I'll have to wear my Sunday best when I go for a ride, and no more rolling in the mud for you, Pippin!" and Pa Bramley chuckled to himself.

Now this made Pippin think. She loved getting dirty and muddy just once in a while.

"If I ride in Ma's new car, I shall have to keep clean all the time," Pippin said out loud. "I wish Pa still had his grubby old truck!"

"So do I, Pippin," agreed Pa, "it will take ages to mend the truck, so we shall both have to keep clean until then."

Suddenly Pippin trotted off into the long grass under an old apple tree.

"We can both ride around on this," cried Pippin, "and we needn't keep clean all the time!"

"Why, it's my rusty old tractor!" laughed Pa. "I'd quite forgotten it was there. It will be perfect when we don't look our best!" and Pa winked at Ma Bramley in her shiny new apple green car.

Dilly Duck's Noisy Nest

Dilly Duck felt very pleased with herself. She had been searching all morning for the perfect place to make a nest and lay her eggs – now she had found it!

So Dilly set to work at once. She collected lots of soft dry grass and some splendid willow twigs, and very soon her nest was complete.

Now the place that Dilly had chosen did seem a bit noisy, especially first thing in the morning. And, strange to say, it never really seemed to get dark at night. But Dilly loved bright lights and she liked to hear sound all around her, so she was perfectly happy sitting on her neat little nest.

Then one warm spring day, after what seemed a very long wait, Dilly's eggs hatched…and there in the nest were six fluffy ducklings. Dilly was delighted!

"Follow me to the stream, little ducklings," quacked Dilly, "and I shall teach you how to swim."

So Dilly gathered together her new family and marched them across the grass. But, dear oh dear, something was wrong! I wonder if you can guess what it was?

Now Dilly was quite a silly duck. She hadn't noticed that she had built her neat little nest in the centre of a traffic island – right in the middle of a busy crossroads!

There was poor Dilly and her six fluffy ducklings standing on the edge of a road full of cars and buses speeding by. How on earth were they going to get across?

Luckily for Dilly, someone had noticed the little family and came to their rescue.

Three busy workmen were digging a deep hole in the road close by. When they saw poor Dilly, they came across straightaway.

Joe put down his drill and stopped all the busy traffic.

John put down his shovel and placed traffic cones across the road.

And Jim put down his pickaxe and led Dilly and her six ducklings to safety. And when they had reached the other side of the road, Jim carefully counted the ducklings… one, two, three, four, five, six… just to make sure that no-one had been left behind.

Safe at last, Dilly and her ducklings hurried down a grassy bank, crossed the park and jumped straight into the stream nearby.

It wasn't very long before Dilly had taught all six ducklings how to swim…one, two, three, four, five, six…just checking!

93